What Would You Do if You Were Left at the Zoo?

Author: Renee Hand
Illustrations: Middy Mathieu

Gypsy Publications

Published in 2012 by Gypsy Publications
Troy, OH 45373, U.S.A.
www.GypsyPublications.com

What Would You Do if You Were Left at the Zoo?
by Renee Hand; illustrated by Middy Mathieu

ISBN 978-1-938768-06-4 (paperback)

Library of Congress Control Number
2012951084

Book edited by Jon Williams
Book designed by Middy Mathieu and Tim Rowe

PRINTED IN THE UNITED STATES OF AMERICA

To my wonderful boys,
Gabriel and Sheldon, who are dedicated to
the preservation of all wildlife.
I Love you so much!

The bus stopped in front of the zoo with a jerk. Sheldon placed his zookeeper hat on his head and adjusted his matching shirt. The doors opened, and he stepped off the last step with excitement.

"Now, hold onto my hand tightly, I don't want to leave you here with all the animals," Mama teased. People began to fill the zoo pathways. Sheldon stopped briefly and glanced up at Mama. "If I were left at the zoo, I know exactly what I would do!" he said excitedly. Then Sheldon led his Mama to the monkeys.

The monkey exhibit was open, with no roof, and no boundaries between the people and animals. Sheldon turned around with fists on his hips, like a superhero. His chest puffed out with joy. "I'm Zookeeper Sheldon, at your service ma'am. " Sheldon bowed, and then quickly rose. "If I were left at the zoo I would stay here and study the monkeys."

"So that would make you..." Mama began.

"A monkey-ologist!"

"And what would a monkey-ologist do all day?" Mama wanted to know.

"Act like a monkey, of course!"

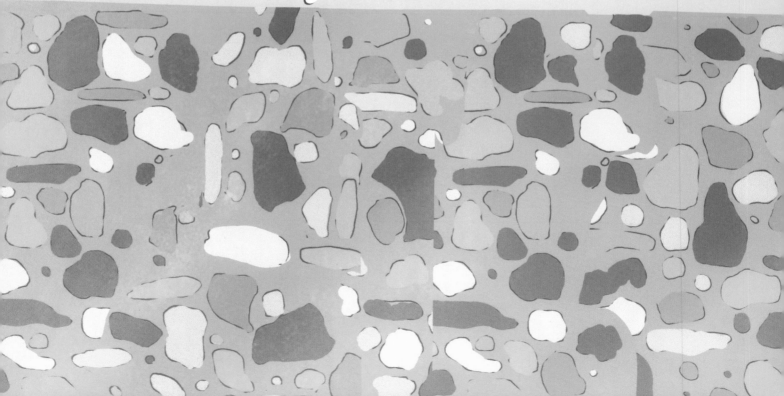

Mama and Sheldon acted like the monkeys, bowing their arms and pretending to swing around, scratching themselves and making, "ooh, ooh, ah, ah!" sounds.

But when a few monkeys began to groom, eating each other's fleas, they shook their heads at Mama and Sheldon, thinking them a silly pair. Laughing, as they swung themselves from their imaginary trees, Sheldon and Mama walked on towards the next exhibit.

They hurried along the path and into the Penguinarium, a building kept cold to protect the various species of penguins that lived within. "I think I will study the penguins instead!" stated Sheldon.

"So that would make you..." Mama prompted.

"A penguin-ologist!"

"And what would a penguin-ologist do all day?"

"Act like a penguin, of course," answered Sheldon.

The little animals in tuxedos almost looked like waiters in disguise. Mama and Sheldon brought their arms to their sides and waddled around the room for some time.

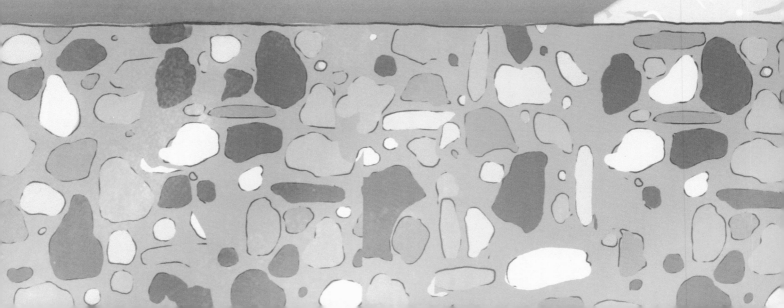

Sheldon even asked mama if she would like some tea. Mama grabbed the imaginary cup, took a sip and continued to waddle. Their laughter filled the room. But the cold air and smelly stench of fish encouraged them to move on with their tour.

Their next stop was the reptile house. Inside was warm and cozy. The reptiles and amphibians were tucked nicely in glass exhibits for all to see. "I think I will study snakes," declared Sheldon.

"So that would make you..." Mama encouraged.

"A snake-ologist!"

"And what would a snake-ologist do all day?"

"Act like a snake, of course."

Mama and Sheldon moved their bodies from side to side as if they were slithering along the ground, hissing as they went. They slithered their way right in front of a python exhibit. The python was enormous, its body wrapped around several tree limbs.

Unexpectedly, it lifted its head and charged forward, hitting its nose upon the glass. Mama and Sheldon's eyes grew wide as they glanced at each other. Then, they quietly slithered their way out the side door.

The next stop was the giraffes! They were tall and slender. The exhibit was filled with green grasses and tall trees for them to nibble on, but that wasn't what they wanted to eat. Wafers were their treat of choice, and people could feed it to them by the dozens on certain days.

"I think I want to study giraffes, even more," spouted Sheldon. "Up close, that is!"

"So that would make you..." Mama pondered.

"A giraffe-ologist!"

"And what would a giraffe-ologist do all day?"

"Act like a **giraffe**, of course."

Sheldon and Mama bought wafers to feed the giraffes. They held out the wafers and the giraffe's long purple tongues curled around the treats as they drew them into their mouths.

Mama and Sheldon moved their necks forward and back as they lumbered their way down the plank back to the pathway and onto their next adventure.

The bear's exhibit was made of rock. It had a water barrier with a steep incline between the pathway and the visitors, so it would be hard for the bears to get out. Sheldon looked at mama and said, "Studying the bears is definitely what I want to do. Their fur looks so soft and cuddly."

"So that would make you..." urged Mama.

"A bear-ologist!"

"And what would a bear-ologist do all day?"

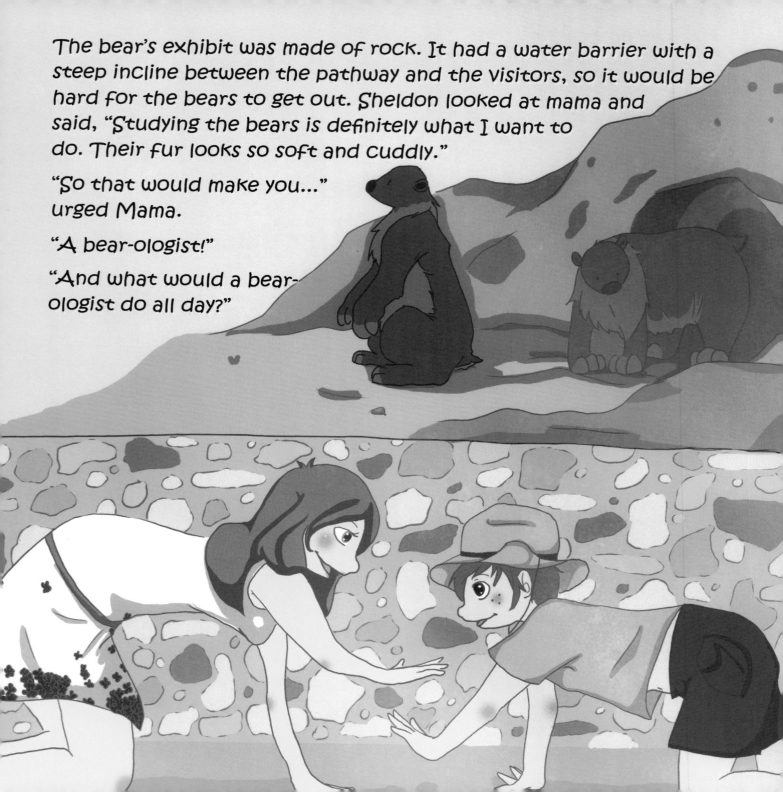

"Act like a **bear**, of course."
"Mama and Sheldon got on all fours and lumbered around like bears, growling here and there as they moved closer to each other.

But one bear didn't seem to understand the pretend play and growled loudly at the pair. Mama and Sheldon rose and stared at the talkative bear. The bear relaxed, then laid back down onto the cool rock. Mama and Sheldon decided to move on and glanced at their map for more fun.

Sheldon had circled the lions on the map as their next stop. The exhibit was filled with lush grasses, down trees for them to climb on, and some shade for them to sleep under.

Golden yellow manes and strong, muscular bodies littered the area as they slept the day away. "Lions are my favorite animal. Studying them would be such fun!"

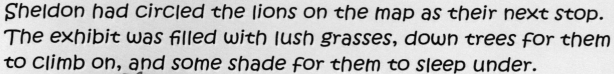

"If you studied the lions that would make you..." inquired Mama.

"A lion-ologist!"

"And what would a lion-ologist do all day?"

"Act like a lion, of course."

The pair raised their arms, pawing the air and roaring loudly. A few of the lions lifted their heads, glanced at them, then rolled over and fell back asleep.

Mama and Sheldon laughed as they had glanced one more time at the lion's sleeping forms before they turned their heads sharply, their gaze landing on an active ostrich playing in the dirt.

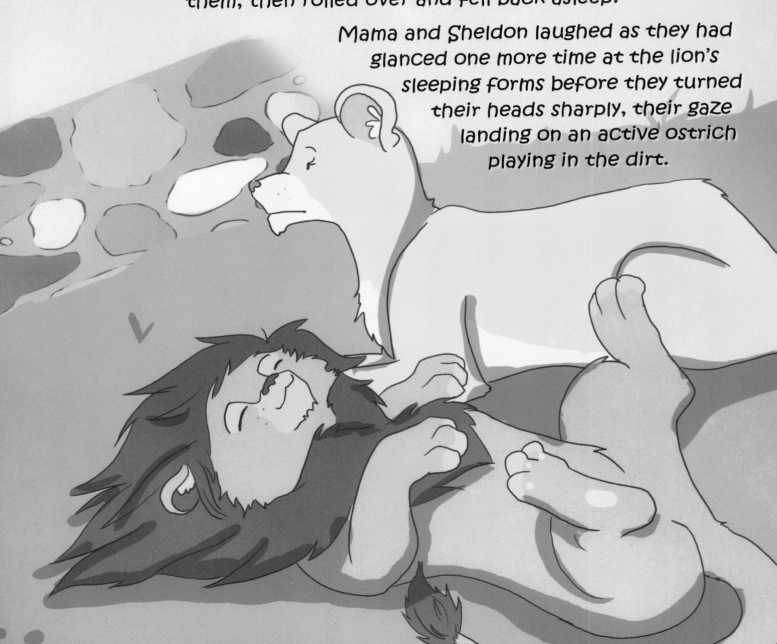

The ostrich was running this way and that, the ground scraped and dug out where it had been.

Eggs, some broken and some whole, were scattered about. Sheldon stared at the ostrich wondering how to copy it, when he saw a worker pushing a wheeled container into the exhibit.

Was it food for the bird to eat? Sheldon got a better look at it as the worker came closer. No, it certainly wasn't food but a container of poo. YUCK!

"So, do you think you want to be an ostrich-ologist?" Mama asked.

"I think I'll pass this time," said Sheldon. Then he waved his hand in front of his nose. While laughing, the pair walked towards the exit, and then out the mighty zoo gates they had entered earlier. They were sad their adventure had come to an end.

Did you figure out which animal you would want to study if you were left at the zoo?" Mama asked as they boarded the bus to leave.

"Mama, I would rather study all the animals at the zoo, not just one. If I did that, I would be a zoologist."

"Cute... but would you really want to be left at the zoo?" Mama couldn't help but ask.

"No, Mama, I would rather come home with you, but the one thing I know is that when I grow up, I want to work at a zoo and become a zookeeper."

"I know you will be a good one," said Mama as she leaned down and kissed Sheldon on the head, squeezing him tightly. As the bus jerked forward, memories flooded their minds reminding them of their adventurous day spent together.

ZOO ACTIVITIES

- Parents or teachers can collect pictures of zoo babies and their mothers before the trip. The children can match each baby to its mother.

- Keep a journal of the animals you see and write down information you learn about them.

- Pick the animal you like best on your trip to the zoo, write a story about it, and then draw it. First, write a description of your specific zoo animal, focusing on its distinctive features. Think about what makes that animal unique. When you are finished, draw a picture of that animal. Use mixed media to make it stand out. Make sure to use a lot of detail in your drawing and your writing. Show feathers or fur, or certain patterns. Then have an art show or presentation to display and talk about everyone's drawings.

- Animals at the zoo come from all over the world. Use a map to keep track of the country or continent that each animal comes from.

- When entering the zoo, pick up a zoo map. As you walk around, mark off all the places you've been. Highlight the ones you like the most and want to visit again.

- Zoos are renowned for helping to preserve species of animals whose habitats are in jeopardy. Think about how you can help save their habitat.

- Act like a zoo animal. In class, every child should act like their favorite animal and see if other students can guess which one they are.

- Take pictures and make collages of the animals and children.

- Keep track of how many animals are herbivores, carnivores, or omnivores. Think of a certain animal's food chain. Who's at the top of the food chain? Who's at the bottom? If a level of the food chain were disrupted, what would happen to the rest of the animals in that food chain?

- Pretend you were a zookeeper for a day. What would be your job responsibilities? What needs would the animals have that you would have to meet? What kind of education would you need?

ANIMAL BINGO

- Create bingo sheets and have students fill in the squares with animals they saw during their trip to the zoo. Place the names of the animals in a container, then draw them.

- Variations could include marking off animals that are reptiles, amphibians, mammals, etc.

CREATING CHARTS AND CLASSIFYING

- Have students write down all of the animals they saw at the zoo. Then have them classify them into groups by making a chart for mammals, birds, reptiles, etc.

- This can be broken down further. You can make a chart for animals that live in water or on land or in trees, for example, or animals that are herbivores, carnivores, or omnivores. Use your imagination.

CPSIA information can be obtained
at www.ICGtesting.com
Printed in the USA
LVIC04n1820090813
347181LV00002B